DESMOND COLE
GHOST PATROL

NEVER A DOLL MOMENT

by Andres Miedoso
illustrated by Victor Rivas

LITTLE SIMON

New York London Toronto Sydney New Delhi

LITTLE SIMON
An imprint of Simon & Schuster Children's Publishing Division
1230 Avenue of the Americas, New York, New York 10020
First Little Simon paperback edition July 2023
Copyright © 2023 by Simon & Schuster, Inc.
Also available in a Little Simon hardcover edition.
All rights reserved, including the right of reproduction in whole or in part in any form.
LITTLE SIMON is a registered trademark of Simon & Schuster, Inc.,
and associated colophon is a trademark of Simon & Schuster, Inc.
For information about special discounts for bulk purchases, please contact
Simon & Schuster Special Sales at 1-866-506-1949 or business@simonandschuster.com.
The Simon & Schuster Speakers Bureau can bring authors to your live event. For more information
or to book an event contact the Simon & Schuster Speakers Bureau at 1-866-248-3049 or
visit our website at www.simonspeakers.com.
Designed by Steve Scott
Manufactured in the United States of America 0623 LAK
2 4 6 8 10 9 7 5 3 1
Library of Congress Cataloging-in-Publication Data
Names: Miedoso, Andres, author. | Rivas, Victor, illustrator.
Title: Never a doll moment / by Andres Miedoso ; illustrated by Victor Rivas.
Description: First Little Simon paperback edition. | New York : Little Simon, 2023.
Series: Desmond Cole ghost patrol ; book 19 | Summary: A slumber party at Grandma
Cole's house turns into a never-sleep-again party when Andres and Desmond discover her
home is full of haunted dolls. | Identifiers: LCCN 2023011271 (print) |
LCCN 2023011272 (ebook) | ISBN 9781665933827 (paperback) | ISBN 9781665933834 (hardcover)
ISBN 9781665933841 (ebook) | Subjects: CYAC: Sleepovers—Fiction. | Dolls—Fiction.
Supernatural—Fiction. | African Americans—Fiction. | Hispanic Americans—Fiction.
Classification: LCC PZ7.1.M518 Ne 2023 (print) | LCC PZ7.1.M518 (ebook)
DDC [Fic]—dc23
LC record available at https://lccn.loc.gov/2023011271
LC ebook record available at https://lccn.loc.gov/2023011272

CONTENTS

CHAPTER ONE

THE SLEEPOVER

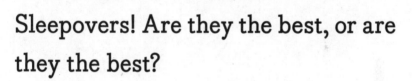

Sleepovers! Are they the best, or are they the best?

I mean, what could be better?

If you've never been to a sleepover, seriously, what are you waiting for? Trust me. You don't know what you're missing.

Like trying to stay awake as late as you can. One time, I stayed up way past ten o'clock at night! My eyeballs felt heavier than bowling balls.

I know what you're thinking. Ten o'clock isn't really all *that* late, but hey, I *love* to sleep.

Plus, there's so much to do at a sleepover.

You play outside until it starts to get dark. Then you play games inside, running all around the house while parents watch boring stuff on TV like the news, old movies, and cooking shows.

But everything changes after dinner. That's when kids get to control the TV!

You know what that means, right? Endless hours of video games, cartoons, and even scary movies.

Well, I don't really watch *those* anymore. Ever since I moved to Kersville, my whole life is a scary movie.

But the best thing about sleepovers are the snacks: chips, cookies, ice cream, cheese balls, *yum*!

At one sleepover, there was a Build Your Own Popcorn Bowl station. I made mine with melted cheese, chocolate chips, caramel, hot fudge, and super-sour gummy worms! And

rainbow sprinkles on top. It was a work of art!

Of course, sleepovers aren't *all* fun and games. I mean, first you have to pack everything!

Which pajamas should you bring? Should you bring your favorite pillow even if it has drool spots all over it?

And what about stuffed animals? There's no way to pick just one!

Then you have to spend the night in a house that's not yours.

That means learning where the bathroom is immediately. Trust me, you don't want to walk into the wrong room at night when you're having an, um, emergency.

Oh, and you'll have to do that *in the dark*!

I mean, who knows what's waiting for you in a strange house in the dark? It could be a cute little kitten. It could be a table leg waiting for you to stumble over it.

Or it could be a whole collection of haunted dolls chasing you and your friend.

Yeah. That's me, trapped in my sleeping bag, squirming like a worm.

And that's my best friend, Desmond Cole, who needs to catch his grandma's vase before it falls and breaks because of two good reasons: (1) that's his grandma's favorite vase, and (2) there could be, like, a

ANDRES MIEDOSO

thousand ghosts trapped inside it. Who knows?

Then there are the creepy dolls chasing us.

Do you want to know what's going on and how we got here?

Me too! All I know is, it started with a phone call.

CHAPTER TWO

THE SECRET PHONE

RRRIIIINNG!!

It was one of those perfect Saturday mornings. I was watching cartoons and eating a giant bowl of cereal when **RRRIIIINNG!!**

A phone rang so loud that I spilled milk and soggy cereal all over myself.

"Mom! Dad! Phone!" I yelled.

But no one answered, and the phone kept ringing.

So I followed the noise to my parents' office. It was coming from the bookcase. Actually, it was a *book* that was ringing!

I touched the book and the bookcase opened like door. There was a phone inside.

My mouth flew open. I'd never seen that before.

Then I did the only thing I could do. I answered the phone. "Hello?"

"Andres Miedoso," said a strange voice. "This is a very important call for your parents. You have three minutes to get them before this call self-destructs."

Self-destructs? Something told me my perfect Saturday morning was over.

If you knew my parents, you would know how much they love to sleep in on a Saturday morning. But how could they sleep through that super-loud phone ringing?

I ran to their room and pounded on the door. "Mom! Dad! The secret phone says it's going to blow up or something! Come quick!"

Within a few seconds they were running out of their room and heading straight to the phone.

I know you're thinking it's not normal to have a secret phone in your house, and you're right.

But my parents work on top secret projects for the government. So we're not the most normal family.

"Yes, we're on the case," my mom said into the phone, then hung up and closed the bookcase door.

"Andres, your mom and I need to go on a work trip," Dad said.

I nodded. My parents took "work trips" all the time. And I knew what that meant. It meant I wasn't invited!

My grandparents usually stayed with me when my parents were away.

It was great! My grandpa cooked on the grill, and my grandma played video games with me. And won!

But something told me my grandparents weren't coming this time, because Mom and Dad were already packing.

Was I going to have to figure out where to go on my own?

CHAPTER THREE

NO INTERNET? NO TV? NO WAY!

With nowhere else to go, I packed my backpack and headed over to Desmond's house. But Desmond was already outside with a backpack of his own.

"Oh no," I said. "Do your parents have an emergency work trip too?"

"I wish," said Desmond. "I have to visit my grandma. She likes me to spend the night at her house at least once a year."

"That sounds cool," I said. "Don't you want to go?"

Desmond shrugged.

"I love my grandma, but her house is SO boring!" he said. "She doesn't even have the Internet. THE INTERNET!"

I'd seen a lot of scary things since I moved to Kersville, but hearing *that* sent a shiver down my spine. A night without the Internet was positively terrifying!

"Well, at least there's TV, right?"
I asked.

But Desmond's eyes told me I was
wrong. "Grandma has an old TV
that only gets three channels. And
they're the *boring* ones!"

"Dude, I'm so sorry," I whispered. "I guess I need to find a new place to stay while my parents are on their secret—wait, I'm not supposed to tell you about that."

"Say no more," Desmond said. "Maybe Zax can babysit you?"

Zax was the ghost who lived in my house. He's a pretty cool ghost, but probably not a good babysitter.

What if he invited all his ghost friends over for a haunted house party? Would there be no bedtime because ghosts never sleep? And what kind of food would Zax make for me . . . spider-egg pizza with extra slime? Ugh.

But then Desmond had an idea. "Dude! You should come to my grandma's house."

"I don't know," I said with a pause. "No Internet, no TV, plus, I don't want to bother your grandma."

"She won't mind," Desmond said. "She loves having young people around."

I didn't have much choice, so I nodded and said, "Okay."

And just then, my parents popped up behind me.

"Thanks, Desmond," Dad said. "We owe you one."

"Have fun, you two," Mom added. "And behave yourself for Desmond's *abuela*, Andres."

Then they jumped into the car and drove off. . . . And I guess that was that. I was headed to Desmond's grandma's house whether I liked it or not.

CHAPTER FOUR

GRANDMA COLE

To be honest, Desmond's grandma's house looked like every grandma's house ever in those fairy tales.

First, the drive to get there was over the river and through the woods, just like in that song!

You know the one!

And the house was old and kind of crooked. My parents would call it charming.

I would call it creepy! I could hear the floorboards creaking before we even went inside. That's how old it was!

Grandma Cole was super-nice though. She scooped both of us up into a huge hug first thing.

"Any friend of my grandson is a grandson of mine!" she said. "Welcome to the family! Now come inside and eat!"

Inside the house actually wasn't as creepy as I thought. But maybe that's because it smelled *delicious*!

One thing I knew about Desmond's parents was that they *cannot* cook. At all! One time his mom made runny eggs with roasted snails and olives, topped with whipped-cream gravy. True story.

But Grandma Cole's house was the complete opposite. There were loads of pies and cakes that had been freshly baked, and everything smelled amazing!

"Aw, Grandma, you didn't have to bake for us," said Desmond.

"Of course I did," said Grandma Cole. "My sweeties always need their sweeties."

Oh yeah. I was gonna like this place.

So we got down to business and attacked that yummy goodness.

Actually, you might want to look away for this part.

Not because it's scary, but because it's kind of gross the way we shoveled food into our mouths.

Sorry, not sorry.

When we finished, Desmond took me to my room. And let me tell you, those floorboards didn't creak at all because I was floating on air with a stomach full of all that YUM. Seriously, nothing could bring me down.

Well, nothing . . . until I walked into my room and saw a bed . . . with dolls on it!

CHAPTER FIVE

ALL THOSE DOLLS

Let me explain. I'm not scared of stuffed animals. I even have some. And no, I don't still sleep with them. Well, not all the time because Zax is always taking them. I guess ghosts love soft cuddly things.

Who knew?

But these weren't stuffed animals. These were *dolls*. Super. Creepy. Dolls. And these dolls had blank faces, with glass eyes that just stared right through you.

"Uh, Desmond," I whispered so the dolls wouldn't hear me.

"I know," he whispered back. "The dolls. My grandma collects them from garage sales or something. You'll get used to them."

I nodded and took a deep breath. He was right. There weren't *that* many dolls. I could do this.

Then I stepped into the room and oh boy! THE DOLLS WERE EVERYWHERE!

"Nope," I said. "I'm not staying in here."

"You can stay in my room then," said Desmond. "It'll be more fun if we're together anyway."

I sighed in relief as we walked down the hall and left those dolls behind. I was starting to relax . . . until Desmond opened another door.

GAH! Desmond's room had *even more dolls* in it! Dolls on the dresser. Dolls on the bookcase. Dolls on the window seat. Dolls everywhere.

Desmond was chill.

But me? I was not chill.

I was frozen. Frozen in fear.

"We can't stay here," I said. "These dolls are made of nightmares."

"They're just silly dolls," Desmond said. "See?"

Then he picked one up and made it wave at me.

But he didn't see what I saw. Because I saw that doll's face totally give me a demonic smile. I could have fainted right then and there, but there was nowhere to fall where I wouldn't land on a doll.

"Is there a doll-free room?" I asked.

"Maybe the basement," Desmond suggested. "Let's check it out!"

That didn't make me feel any better. I mean, basements are the scariest part of any house.

That's why they build them in the
basement!

But Desmond didn't wait for me.
He had already left the room. And
that meant I was there alone . . . with
the dolls!

It was time to have a heart-to-heart talk with these creepy things.

"Hey," I said. "I promise to leave you alone if you promise not to do anything scary. Do we have an agreement?"

Talking to dolls was silly. I knew it. I mean, they couldn't understand what I was saying.

At least that's what I thought.

Because then one doll slowly turned its head and looked directly at me with its empty glass eyes. And it spoke only one word:

"Papa."

CHAPTER SIX

BASEMENT LIFE

I flew out of that room and raced after Desmond. I didn't care how scary the basement might be. Nothing was scarier than a haunted doll.

But guess what? Grandma Cole's basement wasn't scary at all. In fact, it was a pinball paradise down there!

"I told you my grandma likes to collect stuff," said Desmond. "She used to be a pinball pro back in the olden days."

He flipped a switch, and all the machines turned on.

I tried to picture Grandma Cole playing pinball.

Did she have to wear a special outfit like in tennis? Or did pinball pros wear special gloves so they could grip the controls better?

"Are you ready to play?" Desmond asked.

Was I ready to play? Of course I was ready to play!

Who needed the Internet when you had pinball machines? Pulling back the knob and watching the ball fly up the alley and into the playing field. Hearing all the bells and watching everything light up when your ball hits a bumper. It was thrilling!

And when the ball races back down, you have to control the flippers by pressing the buttons on the sides of the machine. You want to keep the balls in the playing field, not in the hole because then the game's over.

Desmond and I played a Wild West
pinball game where the characters
were all tumbleweeds.

It was called Tumbleweed Trouble,
and it was fun!

Then we played one called Underwater Spotter. In that game, we had to launch pinballs at different fish that swam by. Whenever we hit one, it spun around really fast, and it was pretty cool. I can say without a doubt, no real fish were harmed while playing that game.

The next game we played was called Multiball! And it was wild. It had several balls on the playing field at the same time, and eight flippers.

That meant four different buttons on each side. It was so hard, and I was bad at first. But then I started getting better. I was hitting shots that I had no idea how I was making.

"Wow, Andres," said Desmond. "You're super-good. It's like you have more than two hands!"

Hmm, he was right. It *was* like I had more than two hands. Then I looked down at the flipper buttons . . . and my hands weren't the only ones there.

There were creepy doll hands helping me! And the creepy doll hands belonged to even creepier dolls!

Desmond and I jumped back, but we were too terrified to scream. We just watched as the dolls climbed on top of and over the pinball machines. And they all said the same thing over and over.

"Papa. Papa."

"Does this seem normal to you?" I asked Desmond.

"Are you asking if there are always haunted dolls talking to me at my grandma's house?" he asked. "'Cause the answer is no!"

"Then I guess it's time to leave!"
I screamed, and ran away.

But those dolls? They crawled
after us.

CHAPTER SEVEN

HALLWAY DOLL WAY

There's something you should know about me. I don't like climbing stairs. It's work, you know? But you know what I don't like more than climbing stairs?

Being chased upstairs by a pack of haunted dolls!

The dolls were fast. Luckily, Desmond and I were faster. We raced to the top of the stairs and slammed the door shut behind us.

"That was close," I said.

I waited for Desmond to respond, but he didn't say anything . . . which is not like Desmond at all. I looked over at him. But all he did was point down the hall.

My heart did a somersault in my chest.

Desmond Cole is the bravest kid I know. So when he's too scared to say anything, I should have known not to look where he was pointing.

But I looked . . . at a hallway filled
with dolls dragging themselves right
toward us!

"Papa" was all they said.

"Run!" was all I said!

We ran in the other direction and raced into the backyard.

"Good thinking, Andres," Desmond said. "We'll be safe outside."

I looked around Grandma Cole's backyard . . . and yeah, it didn't seem safe.

The grass was tall. There were weeds everywhere. Plus, there was a tree with branches like giant arms ready to grab us. But the scariest part was the old swing that sat in the shadows.

It gave me the creeps.

But we had bigger things to worry about.

I looked back to make sure we weren't followed. Then I said, "Dude, what are we going to do? Those dolls are everywhere. We can't go back in the house again!"

Desmond nodded.

"You're right," he said.

Then he gave me one of his smiles. I'd seen that kind of smile lots of times before, and I knew exactly what it meant.

Desmond Cole had a plan.

Right away, my palms started
to sweat. Desmond's plans weren't
always, um, safe. If we had time, I
could tell you about his worst plans,
but those are other books. And the
one thing we didn't have was time!

"We don't have to go back in the house," Desmond said with a gleam in his eye. "We can sleep in my tree house!"

Then he pointed again.

Remember when I told you about looking where Desmond points? It's never a good idea. But I did it anyway!

I looked up, and up, high into those craggy tree branches, and spotted a rickety old tree house.

It sat on a single branch and looked like it would fall apart in a good breeze. And it was so dusty that I would probably huff and puff and *sneeze* that tree house down!

Then Desmond said the magic words. "I'm sure there are no dolls up there."

And suddenly that broken-down, dusty old tree house sounded like the best place in the world. And guess what. It *was* actually THE BEST PLACE IN THE WORLD!

Let me tell you, the inside was a lot cooler than the outside. It had a library, a refrigerator filled with soda, a cabinet stocked with snacks, and the biggest, softest beanbag chairs I'd ever sat in!

"Why didn't we come here first, Desmond?" I asked.

"I don't know," said Desmond. "I always forget about this place because I usually spend the whole time at my grandma's looking for ghosts. But I never find any."

"Well, you found haunted *dolls* now!" I snapped.

"Yeah, I wasn't expecting that!" said Desmond. "Listen, Andres, why don't you settle in? I'll get you a book and a snack, and then we can finally relax."

I flopped down onto one of the
beanbags and sunk into it.

"Ahhh," I said with a happy sigh.

But I sighed too soon.

CREAK. CREAK.

Those creaking sounds were coming from outside, so naturally I checked to see what was going on. And man, I really need to stop doing that!

Because outside on that old swing was—gulp—a creepy doll. It was swinging back and forth, back and forth, slowly in the wind—except there *wasn't any wind*!

Then its head looked straight up at me and it said . . . you guessed it: "Papa."

Then I heard a new scary sound. It was me . . . screaming!

CHAPTER EIGHT

DOLL-PROOF

Have you ever seen a tree house swarmed by haunted dolls? No?

Well, trust me when I say that you don't want to.

Especially if you and your best friend are the ones who are trapped inside that tree house.

See, one doll on the swing was scary, but the hundreds of dolls climbing up the tree to get us.

Now *that* was terrifying!

Tiny arms and fingers tapped on the windows and knocked from under the floor. The whole tree was covered with dolls crawling closer and closer. And they all had those blank stares and empty eyes. And from their tiny little mouths, they all said the same word over and over again:

"Papa. Papa. Papa."

"These dolls must really think we're their papas, huh?" Desmond asked.

He was trying to solve this mystery the way he always does.

Me? I didn't need to solve the mystery. I just needed to survive until my parents got back from their top secret trip.

"Desmond, we have to get out of here," I said.

"Relax," he responded.

"The dolls can't get in here. This place is doll-proof. Trust me."

Oh, I wanted to trust him, but at that same moment, one of the tiny doll arms punched through the wooden wall and grabbed my hair. Then another one punched through the floor and grabbed my leg!

"The tree house is no longer doll-proof!" I screamed. "THE TREE HOUSE IS NO LONGER DOLL-PROOF!"

"Time for the emergency exit," Desmond said without breaking a sweat.

"Okay!" I yelled as more baby doll arms reached through the walls and the floorboards . . . each with tiny fingers flexing to grab me!

I was sure that Desmond's tree house emergency exit would be dangerous. But when you're hunted by haunted dolls, safety *doesn't* come first.

"Here, put this helmet on," Desmond told me. "Safety first!"

Okay, so I was wrong. Maybe Desmond's escape plan wouldn't be too dangerous after all.

"This zipline goes to the second-floor bathroom in my grandma's house," said Desmond. "I've never done it before. It might be dangerous."

Okay, so I was right the first time.

But there was no choice.

I grabbed hold of the zipline handle and was halfway out the window when Desmond's words hit me.

"Wait," I said, "you've never done this before?"

I wasn't sure if Desmond answered me, because I was already flying out the window.

All I heard was the *zizzing* zip of the zipline and the rush of the wind all around me. For a few seconds it was the funnest thing I'd ever done!

Then I looked down and saw the trail of dolls holding on to my pants.

"No you don't!" I screamed, and kicked my legs.

Those dolls went flying . . . right onto a trampoline I hadn't even seen. And yes, I bet you know what happened next. They bounced right back up and grabbed on to my pants again!

Haunted dolls were hard to shake!
I looked up and saw the open bathroom window, which I was zooming
toward like a bolt of lightning!

WHAM!

I crashed into the bathroom. The
trail of dolls smacked against the
side of the house.

Phew. I took a deep breath. Because there's always one thing you can depend on in a grandma's house. Their bathrooms always have these nice smelling dried flower stuff.

Grandma Cole had a huge bushel of it . . . and I landed right in it.

Then Desmond came flying in right on top of me. Ouch!

That pushed us even farther into the sweet smell. It was so soothing. I found myself yawning. Desmond yawned too. And wouldn't you know it, right there I decided to shut my eyes for just a little nap. I told you, I love to sleep!

And that's just what we did. We fell asleep.

Let's just say, it wasn't the best idea.

CHAPTER NINE

NO SLEEP TILL DESMOND

When you take a nap in a house filled with haunted dolls, you never know where you're going to wake up.

This is something you should remember if it ever happens to you.

I know you're wondering where Desmond and I woke up, right?

Well, we woke up at a tea party. Where else?

But this didn't look like any tea party I'd ever been to before. And yeah, I go to a lot of tea parties. What can I say? I love tea and cookies!

This party was very unusual. The tablecloth was dusty and dirty. The kettle and teacups were all cracked. And worst of all, the cookies were plastic. I know because I bit into one . . . EW!

Another thing: I was trapped in a sleeping bag. Desmond was sitting next to me. And we were surrounded by dolls. Lots and lots of dolls.

"Don't eat the cookies," I warned Desmond, still spitting out plastic pieces.

That was when I noticed the dolls were staring at us. And again, all they said was "Papa."

They said it so many times, the word stopped making sense.

But when the dolls started crawling over the table, that was it. I couldn't take it anymore! It was time to tell Grandma Cole what was going on. Sometimes you need a grown-up's help, especially when there are haunted dolls involved.

So we made a run for it! Desmond was faster, but how fast could I go when I was trapped in a sleeping bag? Not very fast at all!

Oh yeah, are you wondering about the vase with the ghosts in it from the beginning of the story? Don't sweat it.

Luckily, Desmond is great at catching things. Like a cold. And a vase.

Unluckily, those dolls were great at catching things too.

Like super-slow me.

Those dolls crawled all over me until there was nothing left to do but shut my eyes as tight as I could. But then, everything fell silent.

My heart beat loudly as I took a deep breath and opened my eyes.

A doll was looking at me. It's mouth started to move.

"Papa, pa-pa-play with us," it said.

"What?" I asked.

Another doll responded, "Will you . . . Papa, pa-pa-play with us?"

"These dolls aren't haunted," Desmond said. "They're just lonely. They want to play with us because that's what toys and kids do!"

I turned to the dolls and asked, "Shall we have a tea party?"

Have you ever seen haunted dolls jump up and down with joy?

Believe it or not, it's pretty cool.

"We'll bring the tea and cookies," Desmond said, and I could tell he had another bright idea. "You dolls don't know this, but my grandma is the sweetest chef in the whole world!"

CHAPTER TEN

NEVER A DOLL MOMENT

In case you're wondering, the tea party was great.

The dolls were so happy to have kids to play with, and Desmond and I had a great time too.

In fact, we had so much fun we now visit Grandma Cole once a week.

First we feast on cookies, cakes, pies, and whatever else Desmond's grandma makes because she makes the best treats I've ever had. (Please don't tell that to my dad though.)

Then we hang out and play with the dolls. We play everything— cards, board games, hide-and-seek, and pinball of course. We even fixed up that old creaky swing. Turns out, dolls really love to swing.

You learn something new every day!

So, if you ever find a haunted doll in your house, try telling them about Grandma Cole's place and all the dolls that live there. From what I hear, there's always room for one more friend.